Flash's World

Charlie Alexander

Flash's World

By Charlie Alexander

Flash's World

Written by Charlie Alexander

Art Work by Charlie Alexander

Flash jumped into the taxi.

He was on the way to
the airport!

Flying to London.

So exciting!

There's Big Ben.

It's very tall and the clock chimes
are very loud!

It's so nice to cross

London Bridge.

Now on to Ireland!

It sure looks like Saint
Patrick's Day.

Flash was looking for a four leaf clover!

A big red bus made the ride back
to London fun.

Flash liked the seat at the top of the bus!

It was time to leave for Paris.

Flash was crossing the English Channel!

Already in Paris.

It was awesome to see the Arc de Triumph!

The Eiffel Tower stood
straight and tall.

Flash couldn't believe how
lucky he was to see it all!

Denmark was next on the list.

"What a beautiful tulip!" Flash exclaimed!

Wind Mills and Tulips as far as you can see.

It was beautiful and it smelled wonderful too!

A train ride to Germany
spelled lots of fun.

Flash couldn't wait to see where
Ludwig van Beethoven had lived!

It was unbelievable to see all the pictures.

Beethoven was Flash's favorite composer!

This was Flash's favorite picture of all.

He liked the way Beethoven's hair looked!

On the bus heading for Switzerland.

Flash hoped it wouldn't be too cold!

Big ice and snow covered
mountains.

Flash was happy he remembered his hat!

In Spain, Flash saw a bull fight.

Such an adventure. Flash hoped
he'd go to the aquarium next!

Wow! Flash's wish came true.

He loved to see all the fish swim!

Flash really liked the Zebra's
stripes!

The Zebra thought Flash was
cool too!

A helicopter ride to Africa was taking off.

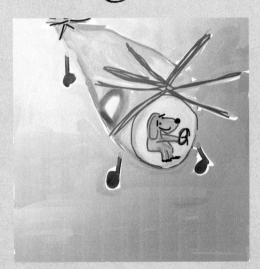

Flash was very anxious to see many different animals!

A friendly Rinausaurus said "Hi" to Flash.

"It's so nice to make new friends!"
Flash remarked!

"What a long neck!" Shouted
Flash when he saw a Giraffe.

He had to lean backwards to see
his eyes!

The Gorilla asked Flash for a banana

But Flash didn't have one!

There were two monkeys who wanted
a banana too.

Flash wished that he'd brought a bunch!

This Camel had two humps.

Flash wanted to take a ride saddled between the humps!

The Lion's roar was so very loud.

It made Flash lay down on his back!

"I like your trunk!" Said Flash.

The Elephant smiled and raised his trunk high in the air!

"See you later Alligator!" shouted Flash.

He was surprised how fast a Gator can swim!

It was time to visit Australia.

Flash had always wanted to meet a
Panda and a Kangaroo!

It was great to make friends with a
Panda Bear.

And the Panda was happy about it too!

The Kangaroo hopped right to it.

Flash really liked the baby Kangaroo!

The Horses were a bonus.

Flash was a little sad to have to leave!

It was time to fly home.

It was heart warming to see the Statue of Liberty!

Back in the USA.

There's no place like home!
The End

To order additional copies of this book, contact:
Xlibris
844-714-8691
www.Xlibris.com
Orders@Xlibris.com

Library of Congress Control Number: 2023902160
ISBN: Softcover   978-1-6698-6582-7
        Hardcover   978-1-6698-6583-4
        EBook   978-1-6698-6581-0

Print information available on the last page

Rev. date: 04/13/2023

Printed in the United States
by Baker & Taylor Publisher Services